S0-CIE-677

Tucson Shooting and Gun Control

A MODERN PERSPECTIVES BOOK

Tamra B. Orr

Published in the United States of America by Cherry Lake Publishing
Ann Arbor, Michigan
www.cherrylakepublishing.com

Content Adviser: Satta Sarmah Hightower, Writer & Editor, Talented Tenth Media, Boston, MA
Reading Adviser: Marla Conn MS, Ed., Literacy specialist, Read-Ability, Inc.

Photo Credits: © Mike Nelson / flickr.com, cover, 1; © Squaredpixels / iStock.com, 4; © Jeramey Lende / Shutterstock.com, 5; ©MCT/Getty Images, 7; © mrdoomits / iStock.com, 9; © asiseeit / iStock.com, 10; © kupicoo / iStock.com, 11; © RyanJLane / iStock.com, 12; © DGLimages / iStock.com, 14; ©Gramper / Thinkstock.com, 15; © Dmcdesign / Dreamstime.com, 17; © Chrisjo88 / Dreamstime.com, 19; © Jose Gil / Shutterstock.com, 20; © pixelheadphoto / iStock.com, 22; © a katz / Shutterstock.com, 23; ©Jonathan Gibby/Getty Images, 25; © Thanamat Somwan / Shutterstock.com, 27; © Ryan Rodrick Beiler / Shutterstock.com, 30

Graphic Element Credits: ©RoyStudioEU/Shutterstock.com, back cover, front cover, multiple interior pages; ©queezz/Shutterstock.com, back cover, front cover, multiple interior pages

Library of Congress Cataloging-in-Publication Data
Names: Orr, Tamra, author.
Title: Tucson shooting and gun control / Tamra B. Orr.
Description: Ann Arbor : Cherry Lake Publishing, 2017. | Series: Modern perspectives | Includes bibliographical references and index.
Identifiers: LCCN 2016058630| ISBN 9781634728652 (hardcover) | ISBN 9781534100435 (paperback) | ISBN 9781634729543 (PDF) | ISBN 9781534101326 (hosted ebook)
Subjects: LCSH: Murder—Arizona—Tucson—History—21st century—Juvenile literature. | Firearms and crime—Arizona—Tucson—History—21st century—Juvenile literature. | Giffords, Gabrielle D. (Gabrielle Dee), 1970—Assassination attempt, 2011—Juvenile literature. | Loughner, Jared Lee, 1988—Juvenile literature. | Gun control—United States—Juvenile literature. | Tucson (Ariz.)—History—21st century—Juvenile literature. | Tucson (Ariz.)—Biography—Juvenile literature.
Classification: LCC HV6534.T8 O77 2017 | DDC 364.152/409791776—dc23
LC record available at https://lccn.loc.gov/2016058630

Cherry Lake Publishing would like to acknowledge the work of The Partnership for 21st Century Skills. Please visit *www.p21.org* for more information.

Printed in the United States of America
Corporate Graphics

Table of Contents

In this book, you will read three different perspectives about the Tucson shooting, which happened on January 8, 2011. While these characters are fictionalized, each perspective is based on real things that happened to real people during and after the shooting. As you'll see, the same event can look different depending on one's point of view.

Chapter 1

Kevin Simpson

Eyewitness

It started with chocolate chip cookies. My daughter Hannah wanted me to make some for her class. "Please, Daddy," she had asked. "Everyone loves your cookies most!" How could I say no to that? Unfortunately, as I gathered the ingredients, I realized I was out of butter. We live only a few blocks from Safeway, so I jumped in the car and headed to the store at La Toscana Village. I had no idea that the small trip would change my life.

After I pulled into the parking lot, I almost decided to go back home. There were virtually no parking spaces available. Why was the store so busy this morning? The holidays were over. Just then, a car backed out of

▲ *The parking lot of the Safeway in La Toscana Village was hosting an event for people to meet state representative Gabrielle Giffords.*

a space, and I grabbed it. As I walked toward Safeway's front doors, I answered my own question. Gabrielle Giffords, our state's **representative**, had recently been sworn in for a third term, and she was holding one of her "Congress on Your Corner" sessions at the store. Already people were gathering to talk to her and tables were being set up. A large banner fluttered in the wind, along with the American and Arizona flags. I had to admit, I'd like to meet her. I thought her ideas on **immigration** were interesting. Maybe if I had more time . . .

Just as I reached the doors, I heard a strange sound. Pop, pop, pop, pop! Was somebody bursting balloons? Some type of publicity stunt to get people's attention? Wait . . . I smelled gunpowder. I turned around to look, and I was horrified. A man in a black hoodie was

Second Source

- Find a second source that provides details about the people who lost their lives in the Safeway shooting.

▲ *Gabrielle Giffords was first elected to the United States House of Representatives in 2006.*

Think About It

- Finish reading this chapter. Why does Kevin Simpson feel he will never be able to eat a chocolate chip cookie again without tears? Give one piece of evidence to support your answer.

holding a gun and shooting into the crowd. I spotted Giffords already on the ground, a young man holding his bare hands against her head. Other people had collapsed and were bleeding. I dropped to the sidewalk and tried to make myself look as small as possible. All I could think of was Hannah looking forward to those cookies.

I peeked through my hands and saw that the gunman had been tackled and was down on the ground. There was a lot of blood, and everyone was screaming. Within seconds, police officers were there, followed by firefighters, ambulances, and three medical helicopters. Giffords was whisked away, and I heard someone say she was in critical condition. She had been shot in the head, and no one was sure if she would survive.

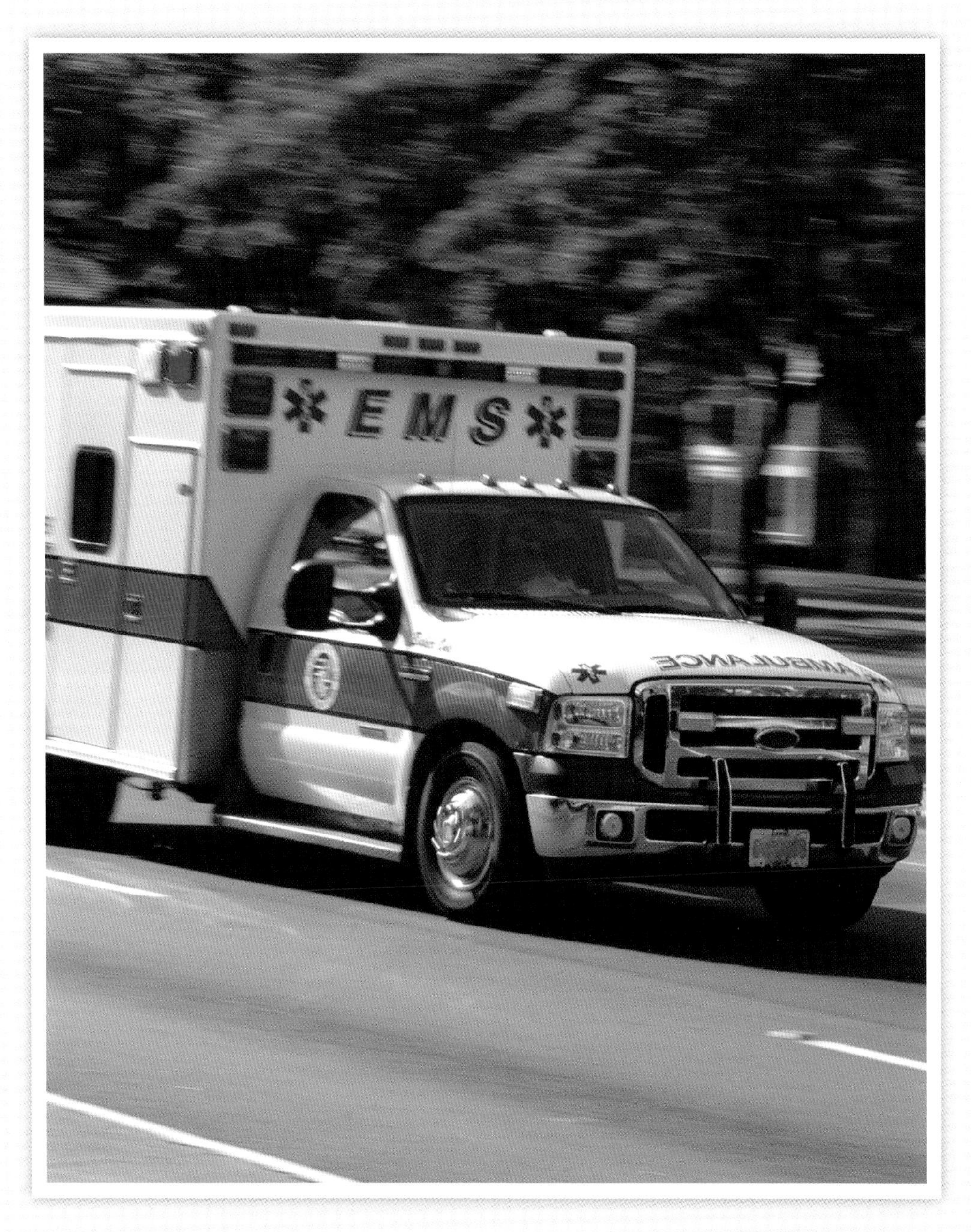

▲ *Emergency responders are trained to act fast in dangerous situations.*

▲ *During an emergency, local news organizations give important updates to citizens.*

For the next hour, I stayed on-site to see if there was anything I could do to help. Nineteen people had been shot, and six of them had died, including a district judge and a young girl who was there to do a school report. Someone in the parking lot had a radio on, and we took time to listen to updates about Giffords. When the reporter stated she was still alive, a huge cheer went up. Gabby, as she was often called, was already being whisked into surgery. I hoped she would be all right.

When I got home later that day, I watched the news about the event. The gunman was in custody, and his name was Jared Lee

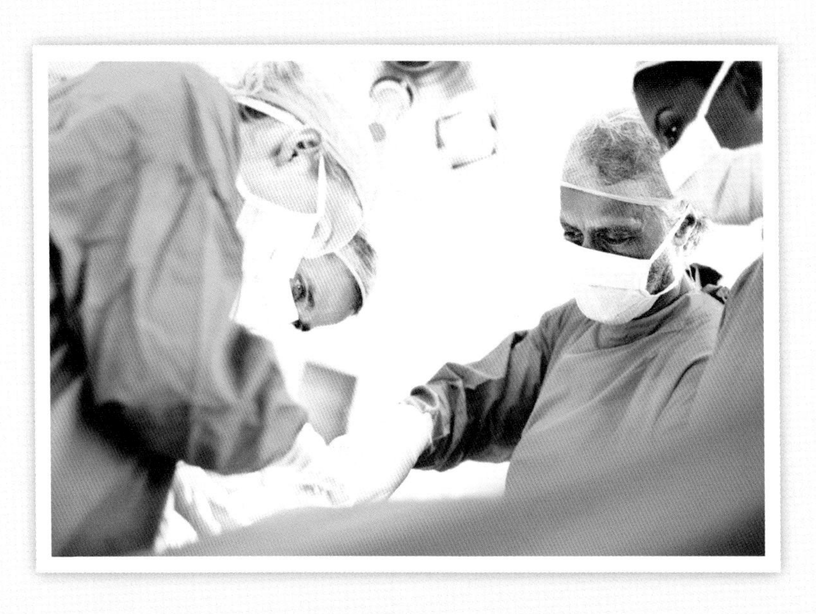

▲ *Giffords had emergency surgery after the shooting, but her survival is credited to a coworker who gave first aid at the scene.*

▲ *People all over the country mourned for those injured and killed in the shooting.*

Loughner. He was only 22 years old. What in the world could have driven him to such violence? I wondered. One thing was sure. I would still make those cookies for Hannah, but I doubted I would ever be able to eat one again without tears.

Tucson Shooting Loss of Life

NAME	AGE
U.S. District Judge, John McCarthy Roll	63
School student, Christina-Taylor Green	9
Pastor, Dorwin Stoddard	76
Dorothy Morris	76
Phyllis Scheck	79
Director of Community Outreach, Gabriel Zimmerman	30

Chapter 2

Samuel Martin

Colorado Student

I grabbed the paper towel and cleaner and started cleaning all the fingerprints and smudges off of the display cases. I went to the wall behind the cash register and dusted off the frame holding a copy of the text of the Second Amendment. I knew it by heart. "A well regulated **Militia**, being necessary to the security of a free State, the right of the people to keep and bear Arms, shall not be **infringed**." My parents had talked about this amendment for as long as I could remember. It was one of the main reasons my dad had opened his gun shop 10 years ago.

▲ *The first 10 amendments to the Constitution are called the Bill of Rights. The Second Amendment gives people the right to own guns.*

"Thanks, Sammy," my father said. I was happy to help any way I could in the shop, especially on days like these when dad looked so distressed. The shooting at the Safeway store last week had been incredibly tragic. I had heard my parents talking late at night about Gabby Giffords and her ongoing struggle to survive. The sadness in their voices was not just for those lost in the shooting, though. A large part of their frustration was due to what this kind of event resulted in: a frantic cry for stronger and better gun control laws. People were writing letters to the newspaper editor, posting their opinions online at blogs and social media sites, calling local and national radio stations, and appearing on

Second Source

▶ Find a second source that explains the details of what the Second Amendment means. Compare the information from that source to the information here.

television shows. Politicians tried to respond, but they never seemed to get anything changed.

"There's another hot debate on CNN," my mom said, pointing at the television. I glanced up and saw two men arguing on-screen. One was a representative of the National Rifle Association (NRA). The other was from the Brady Campaign to Prevent Gun Violence. I didn't turn up the volume. I had heard all of these arguments before.

▲ *Many people fight hard to keep the rights granted to them by the Second Amendment.*

Analyze This

- How is the Martin family's perspective about guns different from people fighting for tighter gun laws?

"I understand why shootings like the one at Safeway frighten people," my mother said. "I just don't understand why they think the solution is limiting access to guns. If more people had been armed in that parking lot, maybe Loughner would have been killed before he got off a single shot." Then she added, "Guns are not for violence—they're for protection."

"And what is more important than owning a gun, Samuel?" my father asked me.

I knew the answer to this one. "Knowing how to—and how NOT to—use it," I replied.

My parents had given my brother, Thomas, and me lessons in gun safety when we turned 10. At 11, we were each given our own rifle and hunting license, so we could go on hunting trips with Dad. So far, I hadn't been able to hit anything, but my aim was getting better. I hoped to get a deer this year.

"Want to do some target shooting this weekend?" Dad asked.

I nodded eagerly. Shooting tin cans and bales of hay was fun, and I always looked forward to it. It helped me get more familiar with my gun and improve my aim. How could a hobby like that be threatening to some people? I wondered. Why would some politician somewhere want to take away my right to have a gun and shoot a few targets?

▲ *Many families know that safety lessons and practice is important for responsible gun ownership.*

▲ *President Barack Obama faced criticism from both gun control advocates and those who supported the NRA, after the shooting in Tucson.*

Glancing up at the wall, I took another look at the Second Amendment. The freedom to "keep and bear Arms" was one I understood and would fight for, even when so many others told me I was wrong. It was my right.

NRA Talks Back

In response to the Tucson shootings, NRA president Wayne LaPierre placed most of the blame on gun control advocates, Obama's administration, and the media. In his speech, he condemned "gun-free zones and anti–self-defense laws that protected the safety of no one except the killers and condemned the victims to death without so much as a prayer." LaPierre stated that passing additional gun laws would make every American less safe and make criminals more dangerous. He added, "Good guys carrying guns can and do make a difference. . . The best way to stop a bad guy with a gun is a good guy with a gun."

Chapter 3

Marian Brown

Vigil Participant

I stood on the University of Arizona campus, along with thousands of others. It was a cold evening, but I didn't mind. I had bundled up so I could stay at the vigil as long as possible.

"Marian, did you hear the bells ring this morning?" my friend Janice asked me.

"I did—right at 10:11 a.m.," I replied. When the citywide bells had started ringing, I was confused. Was one of the churches sending out a message because it was Sunday? Then I realized the date. It had been one year since the shootings in front of Safeway. I remembered that awful day well. My youngest sister, Michelle, had gone to school

▲ *Following a tragedy, communities often hold vigils to remember those who died and support those in recovery.*

Analyze This

- Research the Americans for Responsible Solutions, the committee Gabrielle Giffords founded that calls for stricter gun regulations. How do you think what happened to her influenced her perspective?

with Christina-Taylor Green. It had taken a long time for her to recover from losing a classmate. I was glad that Tucson had named a park after Christina-Taylor.

"Hey! There she is!" Janice shouted, pointing at the **podium** in front of the crowd. One of Gabrielle Giffords's aides, Ron Barber, introduced Gabby with the simple words, "Welcome home, congresswoman." People began cheering as she carefully walked up on the stage. She limped, and her husband, former astronaut Mark Kelly, helped her over to the microphone. Gently, he reached over and helped her place her left hand over her heart. Slowly but clearly, Gabby recited the Pledge of Allegiance, her head held high. "I pledge allegiance to the flag of the United States of America," she said strongly.

▲ *Gabrielle Giffords's appearance at the vigil was inspiring to many.*

Think About It

- Read the statement made by Tucson's mayor. What was his main reason for speaking? Give two reasons why you think this.

When she finished, we all began cheering "Gabby! Gabby!" She pumped her hand in the air and smiled at the crowd. It was an amazing moment. A year ago, none of us would have believed that Giffords would have recovered enough to speak in front of a crowd. The congresswoman had to relearn how to walk and talk. I read that she had undergone months of physical and speech therapy. She had not done many interviews since her shooting, so everyone was absolutely thrilled to see her. Many of us wondered if she would ever return to politics.

Gabby and her husband carefully lit a candle, one of the 19 that were lit to honor all of those people who had been killed or injured in the shooting a year ago. I felt tears running down my face, and, looking around, I saw I wasn't the only one crying. Janice handed me a tissue

▲ *At the vigil, Mayor Jonathan Rothschild called the people of Tucson, "United, compassionate, one million strong."*

and smiled at me. She was upset as well. It was a moment we would always remember.

"Those of us who survived were forever changed by that moment," Kelly said, referring to the shooting. "For the past year, we've had new realities to live with, the reality and pain of letting go of the past. There's a reality that life is unpredictable and that even in the best of times, our cherished friends, the good, the caring, the innocent among us, the closest and dearest people we know, can be taken from us."

When Gabby left the stage, the crowd erupted into applause and calls of, "We need you, Gabby! We love you!" I yelled as loud as anyone.

Tucson's mayor Jonathan Rothschild had spoken earlier. He reminded us to be proud of our city, despite what Jared Lee Loughner had done. "Let us continue to know who we are as a people in Tucson," he said. "United, **compassionate**, one million strong!"

I smiled. A year ago was a tragedy, but tonight was a celebration. I was glad to be a part of it and proud to be a resident of Tucson.

A Long Recovery

In the years since Gabrielle Giffords was shot, she has kept very busy. Along with relearning how to walk and talk, she has also hiked the Grand Canyon, participated in a 40-mile bike race, and skydived. Although she has made a wonderful recovery, Giffords still struggles with paralysis on her right side. Communicating also remains challenging, and she continues to have speech therapy every week.

Look, Look Again

This photo shows a protest against stricter gun laws. Use the image to help you answer the following questions:

1. How would an eyewitness to the Tucson shooting react to this photo?
2. What would a gun owner think about the women in this photo? Would he agree with them? Why or why not?
3. How would a Tucson student feel after seeing this photo? How might that be different if she had attended the vigil for the victims?

Glossary

compassionate (kuhm-PASH-uhn-it) showing sympathy

immigration (im-ih-GRAY-shuhn) the act of entering a new country to settle permanently

infringed (in-FRINJD) interfered in a way that violates the law or the rights of others

militia (muh-LISH-uh) a group of people who are trained to fight but are not professional soldiers

podium (poh-DEE-uhm) small raised platform

representative (rep-rih-ZEN-tuh-tiv) somebody who is chosen to speak or act for others, especially as a member of legislature

Learn More

Further Reading

Houser, Aimee. *Tragedy in Tucson: The Arizona Shooting Rampage*. Minneapolis: ABDO Publishing Co., 2012.
MacKay, Jenny. *Gun Control*. Detroit: Lucent Books, 2013.
Merino, Noel. *Gun Control*. Detroit: Greenhaven Press, 2013.
Obama, Barack. *Three Eulogies: President Barack Obama's Remarks after the Tragedies at Charleston, Newtown, and Tucson*. Create Space, 2015.
Otfinoski, Steven. *Gun Control*. New York: Children's Press, 2014.

Web Sites

KidsHealth—Gun Safety
http://kidshealth.org/en/kids/gun-safety.html

KidzSearch—2011 Tucson Shooting
http://wiki.kidzsearch.com/wiki/2011_Tucson_shooting

NRA Eddie Eagle GunSafe® Program
https://eddieeagle.nra.org

Index

About the Author

Tamra Orr remembers watching the news reports of the shooting on television. She is the author of hundreds of books for readers of all ages. She lives in the Pacific Northwest with her family and spends all of her free time writing letters, reading books, and going camping. She graduated from Ball State University with a degree in English and education and believes she has the best job in the world. It gives her the chance to keep learning all about the world and the people in it.